First published in 2012 by
The Puppet Company Ltd
Units 2–4 Cam Centre
Wilbury Way
Hitchin
Herts
SG4 0TW

www.thepuppetcompany.com

Text copyright © Sue Lockey, 2012
Illustrations copyright © Sandra Evans, 2012

ISBN: 978-1-908633-08-8

British Library Cataloguing-in-Publication Data
A catalogue record for this book is available
from the British Library

Printed in China

The Three Little Pigs

The Three Little Pigs

Re-told by Sue Lockey
Illustrated by Sandra Evans

Once upon a time there were three little pigs who had grown too big to stay with their mother. So they all set off to find houses of their own.

They were excited, but also a little bit scared about doing this, as their mother had warned them to watch out for the Big Bad Wolf.

They waved good-bye and went off on their way.

The first little pig walked along the road, and after a while he met a farmer who was carrying a large bundle of straw.

He thought this would be very good for building his house, so he asked the farmer, "May I please have some straw to build my house with?"

The farmer was a very kind man and replied, "Yes, you may." He gave the little pig a huge bundle of straw.

"Thank you very much," said the little pig. He went and found a flat, clear space to build his house.

He worked very hard, and by the end of the day he had built a beautiful little house. "Now I will be safe from that Big Bad Wolf," he said.

The second little pig walked along the road, and after a while he met a woodcutter who was carrying a large bundle of sticks.

He thought that they would be very good for building his house, so he asked the woodcutter, "May I please have some sticks to build my house with?"

The woodcutter was a very kind man and replied, "Yes, you may." He gave the little pig a huge bundle of sticks.

"Thank you very much," said the little pig. He went and found a flat, clear space to build his house.

He worked very hard, and by the end of the day he had built a beautiful little house. "Now I will be safe from that Big Bad Wolf," he said.

The third little pig walked along the road, and after a while he met a builder who was carrying a large stack of bricks.

He thought that they would be very good for building his house, so he asked the builder, "May I please have some bricks to build my house with?"

The kind builder replied, "Yes, you may."

He gave the little pig a big stack of bricks.

"Thank you very much," said the little pig. He went and found a flat, clear space to build his house.

He worked very hard, and by the end of the day he had built a beautiful little house. "Now I will be safe from that Big Bad Wolf," he said.

Well, early the next morning, the first little pig was woken up by a loud knocking on his door. It was the Big Bad Wolf!

"Little pig, little pig, let me come in, or I'll huff and I'll puff and I'll blow your house down!"

"No, no!" cried the first little pig. "Not by the hair on my chinny chin chin! I will not let you in."

So that naughty Wolf huffed and puffed and blew down the house made of straw.

The poor little pig ran quickly to hide in his brother's house made of sticks, further along the road.

Well, very soon they both heard a very loud knocking on the door. It was that Big Bad Wolf again!

"Little pigs, little pigs, let me come in, or I'll huff and I'll puff and I'll blow your house down!"

"No, no!" cried the second little pig. "Not by the hair on my chinny chin chin! I will not let you in."

So that naughty Wolf huffed and puffed and blew down the house made of sticks.

The poor little pigs ran quickly to hide in their brother's house made of bricks, further along the road.

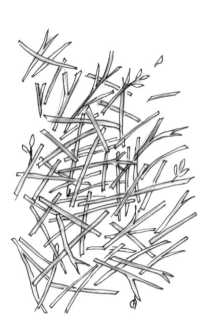

Well, soon after they got there, they all heard a very loud knocking on the door. It was that Big Bad Wolf again!

"Little pigs, little pigs, let me come in, or I'll huff and I'll puff and I'll blow your house down!"

"No, no, no!" shouted the third little pig. "Not by the hair on my chinny chin chin! I will not let you in."

So that naughty Wolf huffed and he puffed, and he puffed and he huffed, and he huffed and he puffed, but he could not blow down the house made of bricks!

"Huh! This is not much fun," he said crossly. "I am going to go somewhere else to find a house that I can blow down!"

So off he went. He never came back to bother the three little pigs again, and they all lived happily ever after in the little house made of bricks.